D1305115

the SMURFS™

THE 100th SMURF

by Peyo

Simon Spotlight

New York **London** **Toronto** **Sydney** **New Delhi**

SIMON SPOTLIGHT

An imprint of Simon & Schuster Children's Publishing Division

1230 Avenue of the Americas, New York, New York 10020

© Peyo - 2003 - Licensed through Lafig Belgium - www.smurf.com.

English language translation copyright © 2012 © Peyo - 2012 - Licensed through Lafig Belgium - www.smurf.com.

All rights reserved. Originally published in French as *Le centième Schtroumpf* written by Peyo. Translated by Elizabeth Barton.

All rights reserved, including the right of reproduction in whole or in part in any form.

SIMON SPOTLIGHT and colophon are registered trademarks of Simon & Schuster, Inc.

For information about special discounts for bulk purchases, please contact Simon & Schuster Special Sales at 1-866-506-1949 or business@simonandschuster.com.

Manufactured in the United States of America   0212 CWM

10 9 8 7 6 5 4 3 2

ISBN 978-1-4424-3615-2

One day the weather
the Land of the Smurfs
anged overnight. Dark
ouds hovered over Smurf
llage, and an evil wind
ook the Smurfs' houses.

Suddenly a gust of wind blew open Vanity Smurf's door. It knocked over his favorite mirror, shattering it into a million pieces.

"Oh no!" cried Vanity Smurf. "This is awful. What will I do without my mirror?"

Meanwhile, Papa Smurf was very worried about the storm. What he read in the Smurf almanac didn't help.

In the 654th year of the Smurf era, an evil wind will be a sign of the start of 100 years of bad luck. The only way to stop this is to perform the Dance of 100 Smurfs.

Papa Smurf shook his head. "This is the 654th year and the wind is frightful . . . but are there 100 Smurfs?"

Quickly, Papa Smurf ran all over Smurf Village, counting Smurfs. But it seemed like the bad luck had already begun. There were all kinds of accidents smurfing around him.

"What will we do?" cried Papa Smurf. "I can only find 99 Smurfs. We can't smurf the dance!"

Meanwhile, Vanity Smurf got to work making an unbreakable mirror out of metal. The noise from his hammering kept the village awake, so Vanity went into the forest to finish his work. "At least I won't bother anyone here!" he said.

Just as Vanity put the finishing touches on his new mirror, heavy rain began to fall. He grabbed his new mirror and ran back toward Smurf Village.

Suddenly a bolt of lightning struck the mirror and threw Vanity Smurf to the ground!

"Phew! It isn't broken," Vanity Smurf said with a sigh, seeing the mirror lying on the ground.

"Broken isn't it. Phew!" repeated his reflection.

Vanity Smurf was confused. "Who is smurfing?" he asked.

"Smurfing is who?" the other Smurf replied.

Then Vanity Smurf realized what had happened: His reflection had come to life!

Vanity Smurf ran to Papa Smurf for help, and his reflection followed.
"So the lightning struck and we became two!" Vanity Smurf explained.
"Two became we and struck lightning the so," the reflection said.

Papa Smurf was shocked . . . but when he realized there was a new
Smurf he shouted with joy. "We have 100 Smurfs! We can smurf the
dance and end this period of bad luck!"

The Smurfs began rehearsing the Dance of 100 Smurfs, but Vanity Smurf's reflection did everything backwards. It was a disaster!

"It's the second Vanity Smurf's fault. He smurfs everything wrong!" yelled a furious Smurf.

Vanity Smurf defended his reflection, but it looked like it would be impossible to smurf the dance.

Vanity Smurf took his reflection home, but that didn't go very well either. They had trouble getting through the doorway, and they hurt themselves trying to sit down for dinner.

It was the worst at night: They pushed each other off the bed!

By morning Vanity Smurf had enough and kicked his reflection out of his house! With the door closed between them, Vanity Smurf's reflection couldn't mirror him anymore. They were free!

The reflection decided to smurf back to the forest. He found the mirror lying in the grass and tried to jump through it so he could go back where he came from— but it didn't work!

All of a sudden a bolt of lightning hit the mirror again, and he was able to cross through the sheet of metal.

At the same time, a group of Smurfs arrived in the clearing. They had gone looking for Vanity Smurf's reflection to ask him to come back to the village.

"I don't know what just smurfed," the reflection said. "But I think I went through the mirror!"

"He smurfs normally!" cried Papa Smurf. "He has become a real Smurf!"

That night the Smurfs were finally able to perform the Dance of 100 Smurfs. The period of bad luck came to an end . . . all thanks to Vanity Smurf's reflection, the 100th Smurf.